BOO BOO

SPOOKTACULAR TALES

by
Benjamin Bird
Michael Dahl
John Sazaklis

illustrated by
Patrycja Fabicka

PICTURE WINDOW BOOKS
a capstone imprint

Boo Books is published by
Picture Window Books, a Capstone Imprint
1710 Roe Crest Drive
North Mankato, Minnesota 56003
capstonepub.com

Library of Congress Cataloging-in-Publication Data is available
on the Library of Congress website

ISBN: 9781484686423 (paperback)
ISBN: 9781484686430 (ebook PDF)

Summary: Looking for scary (but not too scary) stories? This collection
of tales puts eerie monsters in familiar settings to creep out a rotating
cast of characters. From gooey blob monsters and video games of doom
to chilling clowns and swamp creature teachers, these four stories
deliver just-right frights without the sleepless nights.

Design Elements: Shutterstock: ALEXEY GRIGOREV, design element,
vavectors, design element, Zaie, design element

Designers: Sarah Bennett and Bob Lentz

Printed and bound in China. 5557

TABLE OF CONTENTS

STORY ONE
CLOWNS FROM OUTER SPACE

by Michael Dahl

illustrated by Patrycja Fabicka

CHAPTER ONE
THE BIG PARTY

It was dark—darker than usual. Ella held a birthday present tightly in her hand. It was for her best friend, Tia.

The present's wrapping paper was bright green. It reminded Ella of something she had seen last night. A strange green light had moved across the sky. She had thought it was an alien spaceship.

But Ella knew that couldn't be true. She looked up in the sky, shook her head, and smiled. It was just her imagination.

Ella knocked and knocked on
Tia's door. She waited. Then she
knocked again.

Tia finally opened the door.

"Ella! You made it!" Tia screamed, grabbing Ella and giving her a giant hug.

"You know I wouldn't miss your birthday party," Ella said.

"This will be the best and biggest party ever!" Tia said with a smile.

I hope there aren't any clowns at this party, thought Ella.

Ella did not like clowns. She thought they looked creepy. And they smiled too big and too much. It was weird.

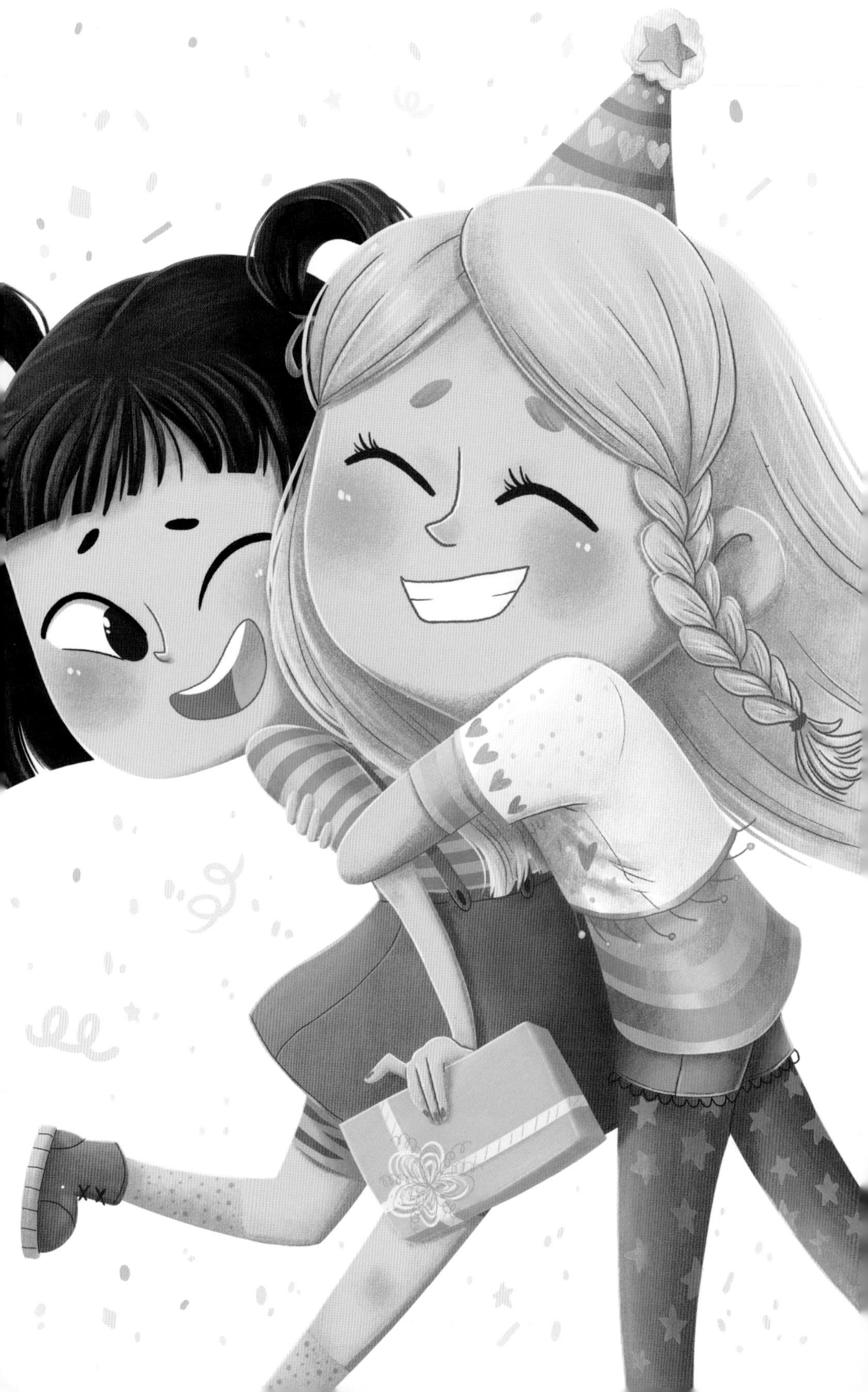

Tia led Ella to the backyard.
The yard was full of kids and
parents and pets and a gigantic
bouncy castle!

CHAPTER TWO

THE CLOWNS AND THE CASTLE

Ella could see kids inside the castle. Through the screen walls she watched them laugh and bounce.

HAAAAA! HEEE HEEEEE! AAAAHHHH!

Then Ella saw something else
inside the bouncy castle. Clowns!
Lots and lots of smiling clowns.

Some of the kids were laughing.
Some of them were screaming.
I'd scream too, thought Ella.

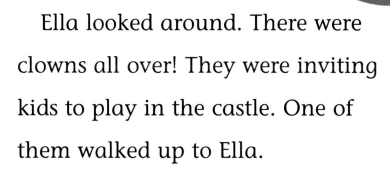

Ella looked around. There were clowns all over! They were inviting kids to play in the castle. One of them walked up to Ella.

"Hello, young lady," said the clown. "Come join us."

"No way!"
Ella shouted.

She ran away
and hid under
the food table.

*This party is
not much fun.
Where is Tia?*
Ella wondered.

"Ella!" shouted
a voice. It was Tia!
She was already inside the
castle and calling to her.

Ella watched as more and
more kids ran toward the castle.

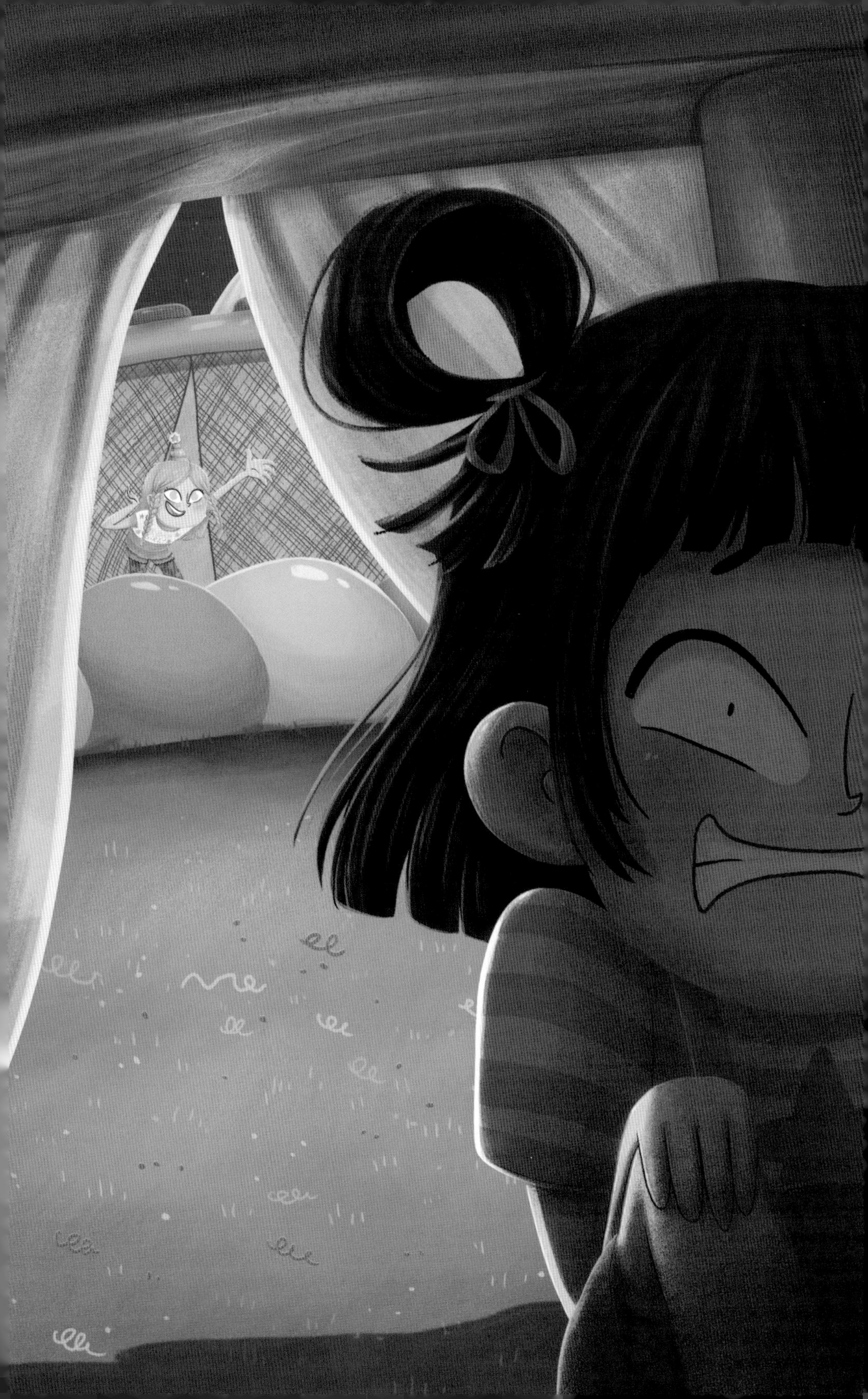

Clowns led the children up the
bouncy steps. Then they pushed
them inside with a laugh. More
kids bounced and screamed. The
castle was getting quite full.

Outside the castle, the parents laughed and waved at their kids.

"They're having so much fun," said one of the dads.

A mom standing next to him had a strange look in her eyes.

"They are! We should have fun too," she said.

The parents stopped laughing. One by one, the moms and dads walked toward the castle. The clowns led them up the stairs and through the door.

The castle was stuffed with people. Ella worried that the castle would burst. Tia ran out of the castle to Ella.

"Come on," she said. "You're the last one left."

CHAPTER THREE

LIFTOFF!

The ground shook. *RUMMMBLE!*
The bouncy castle turned into a
rocket!

The people inside the castle were
still bouncing up and down. They
didn't seem to notice!

The rocket's jets glowed bright green. A mighty wind blew from the bottom of the bouncy castle. Slowly, the castle rose into the air, taking all the guests with it.

"It's an alien spaceship!" shouted Ella.

"No, it's a clown ship!" shouted Tia. "And it's perfect!"

The wind blew
through the
backyard. Tables
were knocked
over. Cake and
ice cream flew
through the air.
The birthday food
splashed all over
the two friends.

The girls watched the rocket soar into the sky. Suddenly, Tia burst into tears.

"I'm sorry the clowns took all your friends and family," Ella said.

"I'm not sorry about that," said Tia. "I'm sorry we missed the ride!"

Tia looked up at the sky and
shouted. "Come baaaaaaaacck!"

Ella looked up. A strange green
light moved across the sky. She
looked over at Tia.

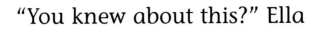

"You knew about this?" Ella
asked.

Tia just smiled.

STORY TWO

GAME OVER

by Benjamin Bird
illustrated by Patrycja Fabicka

CHAPTER ONE
PRESS START

A boy raced through a long, brick maze.

"HUFF! HUFF!"

He struggled to breathe, but the boy could not rest. Something was chasing him.

The boy heard heavy footsteps close by.

THOMP! THOMP! THOMP!

He sped around a sharp corner and came face-to-face with a giant beast!

The monster showed its sharp fangs.

"ROOAAAAR!"

Arthur screamed in his basement. He threw his video game controller onto the carpet. The game's final boss had beaten him again.

"I'll never defeat the Maze Monster!" Arthur whined.

Arthur pressed the game's POWER button, but the machine wouldn't turn off. He pushed the button again—and then again.

An alert popped up on the TV screen. It read: YOU HAVE ONE LIFE REMAINING.

Arthur scratched his head, confused.

How did I get an extra life? he wondered.

Then another message flickered on the screen: PRESS START TO CONTINUE . . . IF YOU DARE!

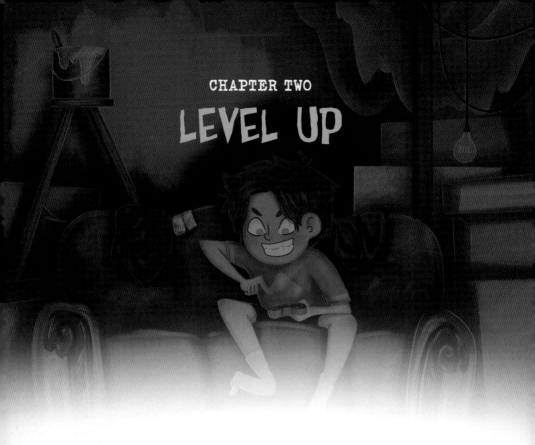

CHAPTER TWO
LEVEL UP

"Awesome! A bonus life!" Arthur smiled with delight.

A countdown began on the TV: "5 . . . 4 . . . 3 . . . 2 . . ."

With one second left, Arthur jammed his thumb on the START button.

CLICK! Suddenly, everything went dark.

"Mom!" Arthur yelled upstairs. "The power is out again!"

But nobody answered.

Arthur grunted. "I sure hope my game saved."

Arthur stood and stumbled through the dark. He searched for a light switch. He didn't find one.

Instead, Arthur tripped and fell. The basement floor felt like brick.

"Ouch!" he cried.

The floor was brick! When Arthur looked up, a bunch of arrows glowed in front of him.

The arrows pointed toward
a steel door marked with
two words: FINAL BOSS!
"What is happening?"
Arthur asked, puzzled.

FWOOSH! The door flung open. Arthur got up, brushed off, and walked through the entrance. An endless maze awaited him.

It can't be, thought Arthur, looking around. *I'm in the video game!*

WHAM! The steel door slammed shut behind him. Everything went silent. Then Arthur heard a sound from within the maze.

THOMP! THOMP! THOMP!

"The Maze Monster!" he cried.

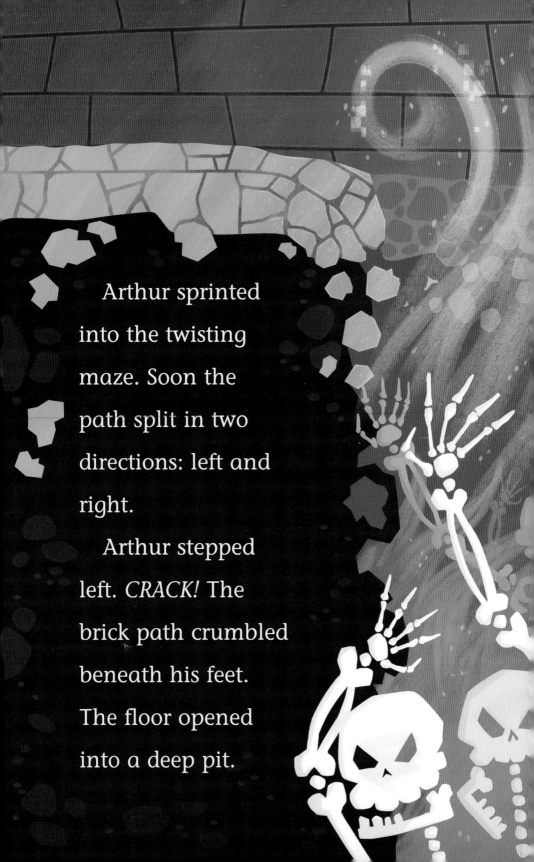

Arthur sprinted into the twisting maze. Soon the path split in two directions: left and right.

Arthur stepped left. *CRACK!* The brick path crumbled beneath his feet. The floor opened into a deep pit.

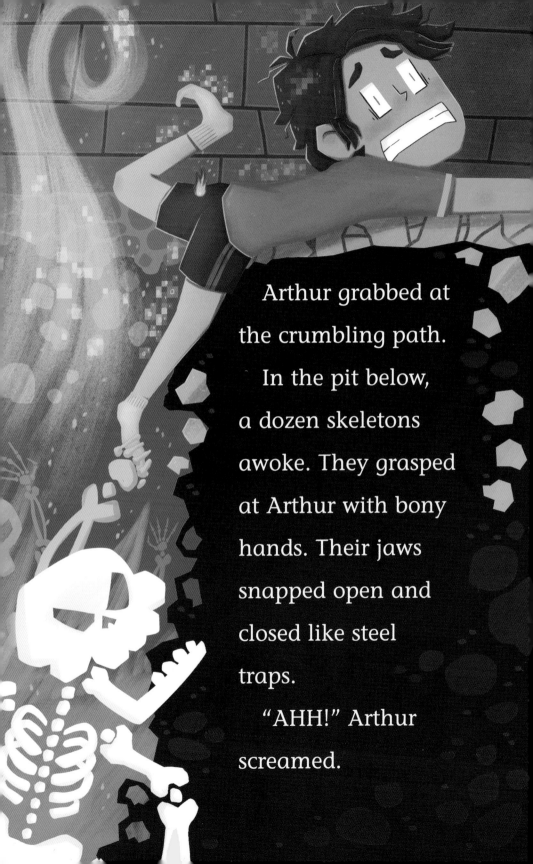

Arthur grabbed at the crumbling path. In the pit below, a dozen skeletons awoke. They grasped at Arthur with bony hands. Their jaws snapped open and closed like steel traps.

"AHH!" Arthur screamed.

CHAPTER THREE
FINAL BOSS

Arthur pulled himself up and crawled safely away from the pit.

"Rookie mistake," he said, shaking his head.

Arthur looked around again.

"Think," he told himself. "You've played this level before."

This time, Arthur headed right instead of left. The floor did not crumble.

As he ran, Arthur remembered the correct path. But with each twist and turn, the footsteps grew louder.

THOMP! THOMP! THOMP!

Then, up ahead, the path turned
sharply. Arthur stopped.

The footsteps stopped too.

Arthur pressed his back against
the brick wall. He inched closer
to the turn.

He could hear the Maze Monster
breathing around the corner.

Suddenly, one of the bricks on the wall moved. Arthur pushed on it, and a secret drawer opened.

He reached inside and pulled out a flaming sword!

"Power up!" Arthur exclaimed.

With the sword, Arthur turned
the corner. He came face to face
with the giant beast again.

SLASH! Arthur swung his sword
at the monster.

FWOOSH! The beast lashed out
with its claws.

The fighting went on. And on. And on.

Both Arthur and the Maze Monster were growing weak. One final blow would destroy either one of them.

SLASH! FWOOSH!

Then, suddenly, everything went dark again.

Back in the basement, a door slowly opened.

CREAK!

Arthur's mother yelled down, "Is everything okay, Arthur?"

No one answered. But on the TV screen, a final message flashed: GAME OVER.

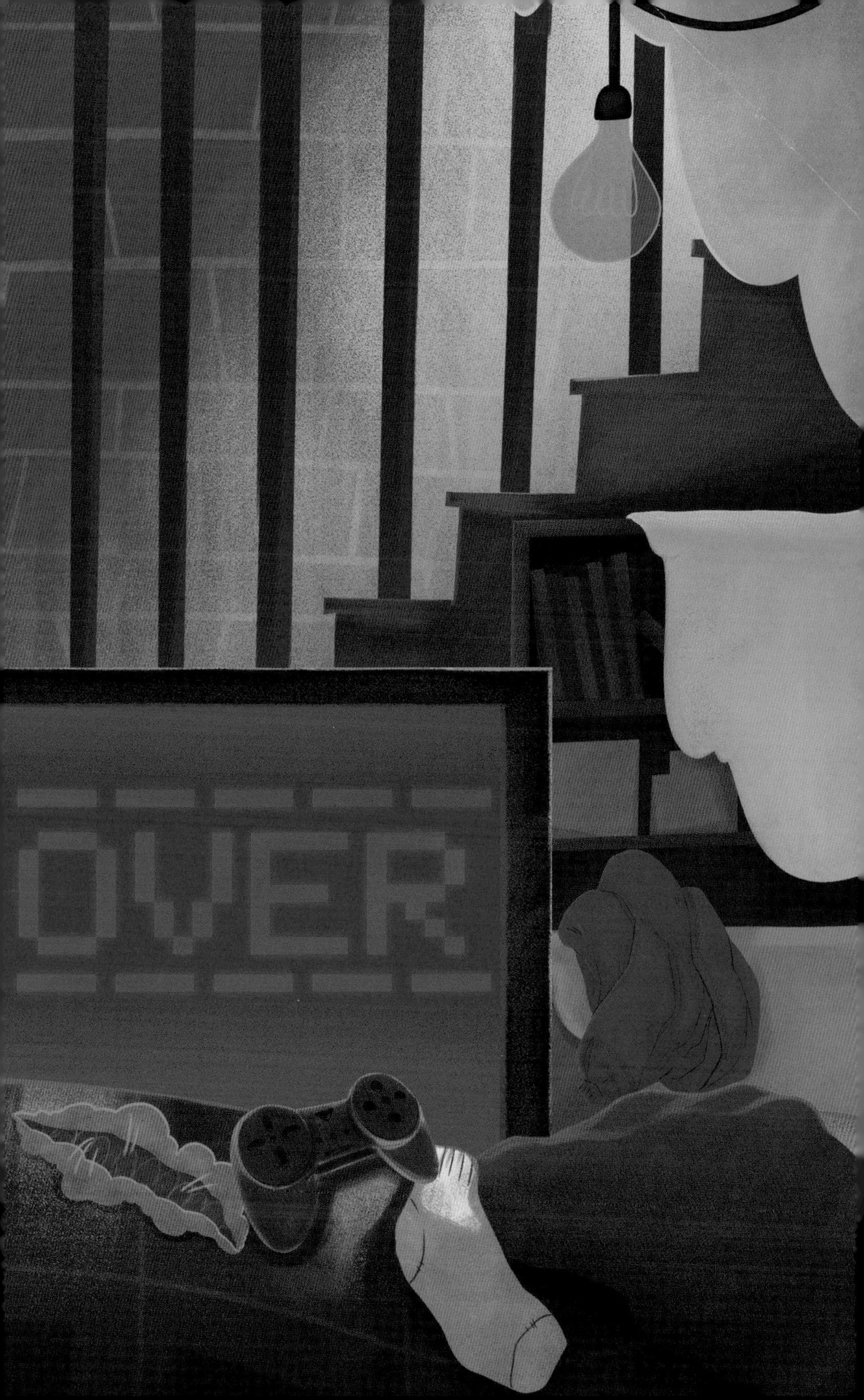
OVER

STORY THREE

SLIME TIME!

by John Sazaklis
illustrated by Patrycja Fabicka

CHAPTER ONE
SNACK ATTACK

"All aboard! We are about to set sail," the captain announced.

Sam had never been on a cruise ship before.

"I can't wait to explore," she said. "There are twelve decks on this ship, and half of them have food!"

"There will be plenty of time to do that after we settle in," her dad replied.

"There's no way I can wait. The all-you-can-eat buffet just opened," Sam said. "And I want to eat while I'm still young! See ya!"

ALL YOU CAN EAT!
Buffet

Sam squeezed herself into the
dining hall. She zoomed straight
for the pastries. She got a huge jelly
donut topped with frosting.

Sam took the biggest bite she
could and quickly spit it out.

"BLAH!" she cried. "This tastes
like slime!"

"How do you know what slime
tastes like?" a red-haired lady asked.

"How do you *not*?" Sam replied.

Suddenly, the splattered jelly on the floor began to move. It reached up and wrapped around Sam's arm and leg.

"Help!" hollered Sam. "The jelly is alive, and it's going to eat me!"

SO. MUCH. SLIME.

"Drop the donut!" the lady yelled.

Sam let it go, and the slime slid off her. But then it latched onto the dropped donut. Sam watched the jelly blob gobble up the donut.

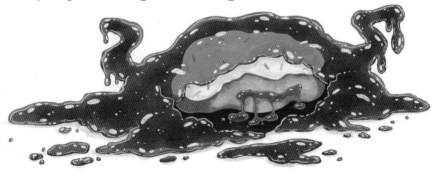

The blob grew bigger and bigger and bigger.

"Whoa," Sam said. "And I thought *I* was hungry!"

The blob grew
two tentacles out of
its goopy side. Then
it started to rise.

Thinking quickly,
Sam snatched
another snack
and threw it
across the room.

"Fetch!" she
cried.

Leaving a trail of jelly goo, the
blob slithered toward the treat.

"Run for your lives!" Sam yelled
as she ran out of the room.

The diners ignored her and
continued stuffing their faces.

Suddenly, there
was a loud sound.
HOOOOONK!
Sam thought
the ship was
blowing its horn.
But that was not
it. Instead, it was
a new, bigger blob
blowing her nose.

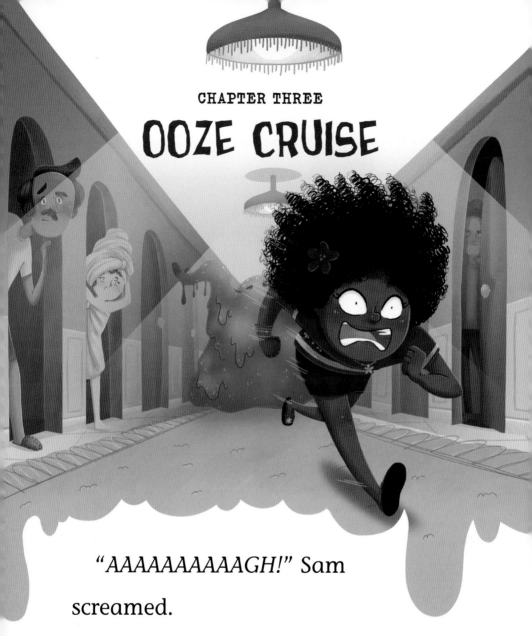

CHAPTER THREE
OOZE CRUISE

"AAAAAAAAAGH!" Sam

screamed.

HOOOOOOOOOONK!

The big blob blubbered again.

Sam turned on her heels and ran

in the other direction.

Oh no! The path was blocked by another giant blob.

"I'm surrounded by big, slimy blobs!" Sam shouted.

She was trapped. The only place to go was back to the buffet.

Back at the buffet, Sam was shocked by what she saw.

Piles of food and globs of slime were splattered around a very angry mob.

The original blob was nowhere to be found.

"There's the culprit! This is all her fault!" the red-haired lady shouted, pointing at Sam.

Just then, the room went dark. People screamed. All around them, thick, slimy ooze dripped through the portholes and down the walls.

The ooze slid into the middle of the room and became two separate shapes. The shapes turned into the big blobs Sam had seen in the hallway!

The blobs let out a loud, rumbling sound.

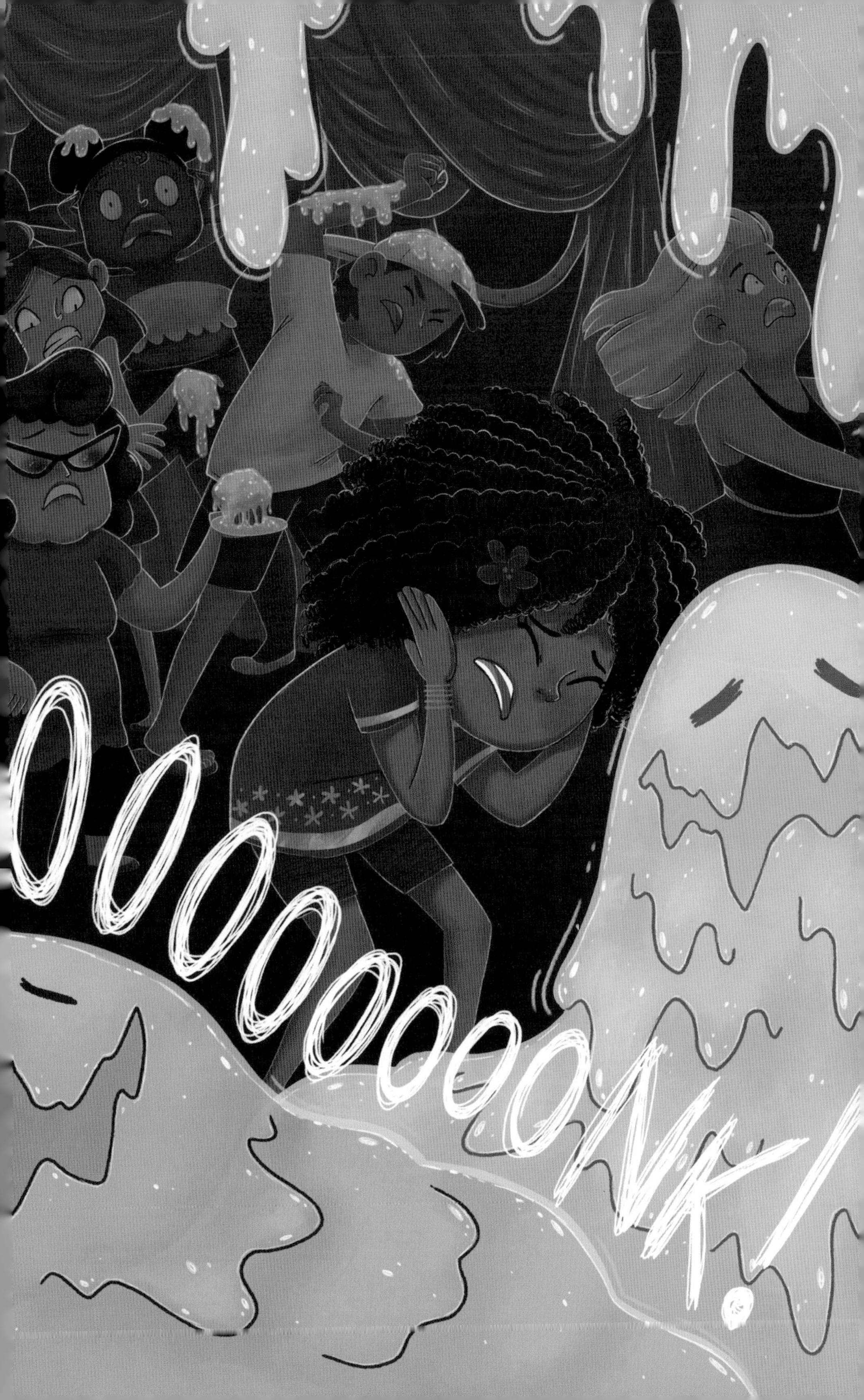
OOOOOOOOONK!

Just then, the original little blob came out from under a table. With a high-pitched squeal, it slithered over to the big blobs.

Their tentacles twisted around each other in a big blob hug.

Sam was still in shock when the captain entered the dining room.

"Sorry, everyone. These worried parents were just looking for their child," she said. "Thankfully they've found each other!"

The three blobs let out a series
of gurgles and burbles.

"How wonderful!" replied the
captain. "They've offered to clean
up this mess!"

The blobs opened their mouths wider and wider. *SLUUUUUURRP!* In an instant, they were done cleaning.

The blobs belched loudly and oozed out a porthole. At that moment, Sam's dad walked in.

"There you are!" he said. "I'm starving."

Then he looked around. Not only was all the food gone, but so were the cups, plates, napkins, silverware, and buffet table!

"Wow," said Sam's dad. "When they say 'all-you-can-eat,' they really mean it."

"You have no idea!" Sam replied.

STORY FOUR
SWAMP CREATURE TEACHER

by John Sazaklis
illustrated by Patrycja Fabicka

CHAPTER ONE
SOMETHING FISHY

It was a hot and humid day
at Murky Meadows Elementary
School. The kids in Mrs. Markela's
class were waiting for their teacher.
But she never showed up.

Suddenly, a tall, thin stranger entered. She had big bug eyes and puffy lips. She was dripping all over.

MRS. GILMAN

Drip. Drip. Drip.

"I am your substitute teacher, Mrs. Gilman," she said.

Two boys named Joey and
Johnny were sitting in the back.
Joey pointed to the puddle under
Mrs. Gilman.

"Look how sweaty she is! She
must be really nervous," whispered
Joey.

"I don't think she's human,"
Johnny replied.

Joey's eyes went wide. "What do you mean?" he asked.

Johnny pulled out a comic book. "She looks just like this," he said. "And our school is next to a swamp. It makes sense."

"What's going on back there?" the teacher asked.

"Something fishy!" answered Johnny, holding up the book.

The students laughed.

Mrs. Gilman came face-to-face with Johnny.

"Not in my class," she hissed and snatched the book away.

CHAPTER TWO

SWAMPED

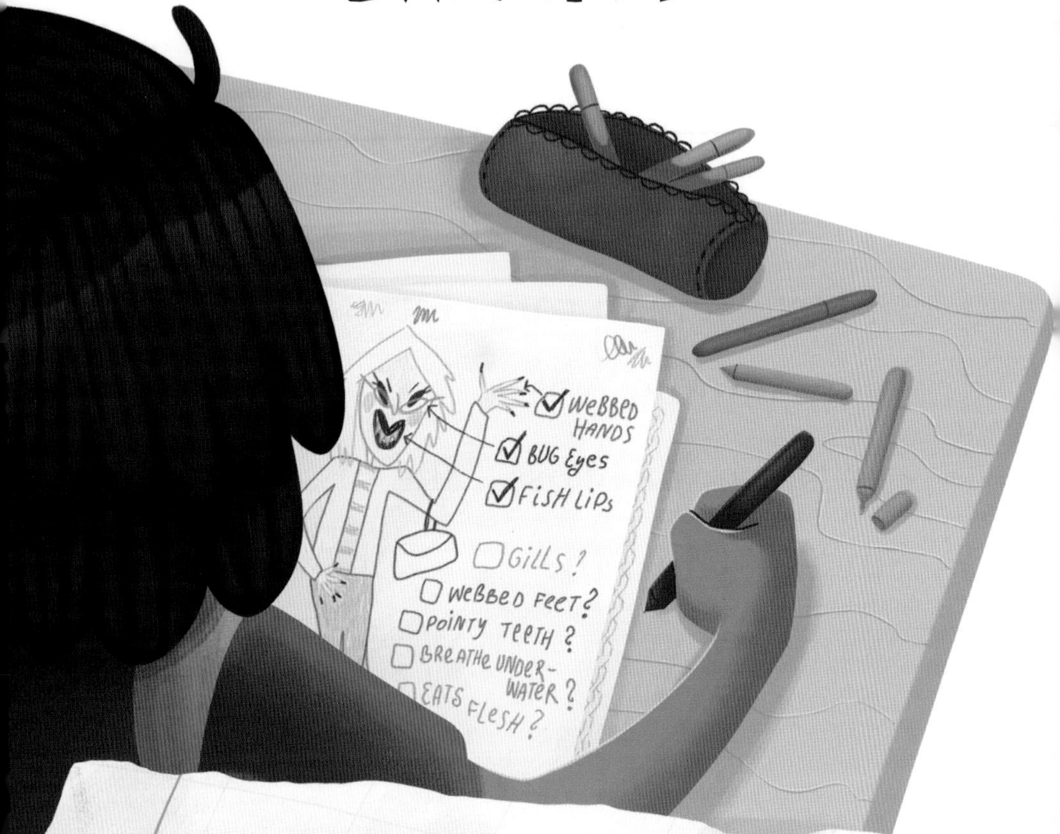
WEBBED HANDS
BUG EYES
FISH LIPS
GILLS?
WEBBED FEET?
POINTY TEETH?
BREATHE UNDER-WATER?
EATS FLESH?

The morning dragged on. Johnny spent it doodling in his notebook. He was sure Mrs. Gilman was a swamp creature. But how could he prove it?

Finally it was time for lunch.

"Off with you, kids," Mrs. Gilman said. "I need to eat in peace."

Once she was alone, she dunked her head into the fish tank.

SPLASH!

Mrs. Gilman was enjoying her lunch when someone knocked on the door.

KNOCK! KNOCK!

She didn't hear anyone until it was too late.

"What are you doing?" yelled Johnny.

Mrs. Gilman pulled her head out of the tank.

"Cooling off from the heat," replied Mrs. Gilman. "I'm feeling a bit swamped!"

Then she cackled. Johnny saw a mouth full of very sharp, very pointy teeth.

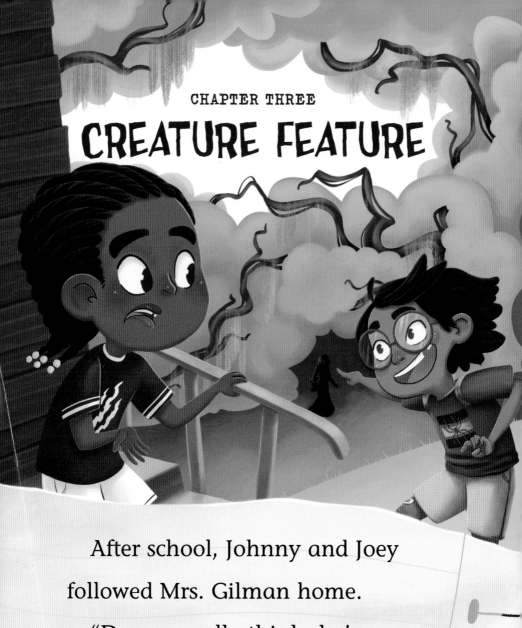

CHAPTER THREE
CREATURE FEATURE

After school, Johnny and Joey
followed Mrs. Gilman home.

"Do you really think she's a
swamp monster?" Joey asked.

"There's only one way to find
out," said Johnny. "Let's go!"

The boys didn't have to go very far. Mrs. Gilman stopped at the swamp near the school. She quickly looked around. Then she walked right into it!

"I knew it!" Johnny cried. "Come on, Joey!"

The best friends crept closer to
the swamp. They did not see a large
figure coming up behind them.

"GOTCHA!" boomed a deep voice.

Towering over them was something
out of a comic book. Only it was real!

"Swamp creature!" the boys screamed.

The monster lifted them high
and growled. "What are you doing
in my home?"

"Please don't eat us!" Joey cried.
"It was all his idea!"

"Hey!" Johnny shouted.

Just then Mrs. Gilman bubbled out of the swamp. "I see you've met some of my students, honey."

"Students?" asked the monster as he dropped the boys.

"Honey?" they replied wide-eyed.

"Yes, boys," said the teacher. "This is my husband."

The boys were speechless.

"The name's Finn. Pleased to meet you," the creature said.

He held out a webbed hand. It was slimy and wet. Johnny shook it. Joey did not.

Mrs. Gilman pulled out Johnny's comic book.

"Hey! That's Finn on the cover!" Johnny exclaimed.

"I thought I would surprise you and get it autographed," Mrs. Gilman said.

She gave it to Finn. He stamped it with his webbed hand, leaving a slimy handprint.

"I can't believe they're real swamp creatures," Joey whispered.

"I told you so," Johnny replied. "And you are holding the proof!"

"Would you like to stay for dinner?" asked Mrs. Gilman.

"Sure," said Joey. "What are you having?"

The swamp creatures flashed
their pointy teeth and shouted,
"YOU!"

"Help! Swamp creatures!" the boys hollered as they ran away.

Finn picked up the comic book that Johnny had dropped and took a bite out of it.

"That never gets old," he said.

"Do you think anyone will believe them?" asked Mrs. Gilman.

"They never do," said Finn.

The swamp creatures laughed and dove into their underwater home for a relaxing night.

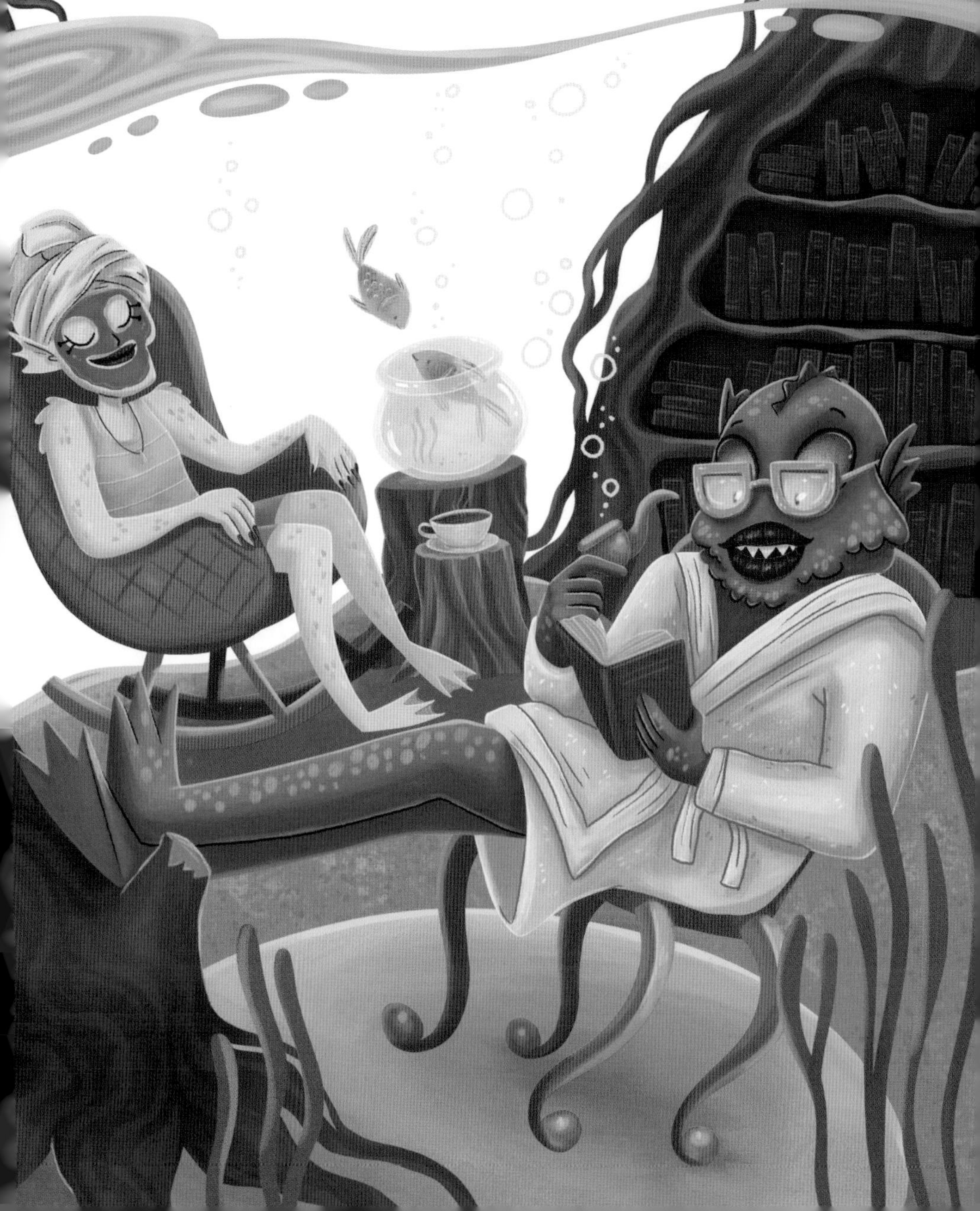

SCARED SILLY JOKES!

Why don't sharks like to eat clowns?
They taste funny!

Did you hear about the clown who worked as the human cannonball?
He got fired!

What kind of vehicle does the Maze Monster drive?
A monster truck

What is the Maze Monster's favorite snack?
Ghoul Scout cookies

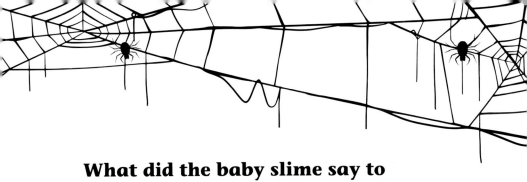

What did the baby slime say to its parents?

Goo-goo!

What is slime's favorite game?

Slimon Says

If fish lived on land, which country would they live in?

Finland

What do fish need to stay healthy?

Vitamin sea

Benjamin Bird

Benjamin Bird is a children's book editor and freelance writer from St. Paul, Minnesota. He has written books about some of today's most popular characters, including Batman, Superman, Wonder Woman, Scooby-Doo, Tom & Jerry, and many more.

Michael Dahl

Michael Dahl is the prolific author of more than 200 books for children and young adults, including graphic novels, the Library of Doom adventure series, the Dragonblood books, Trollhunters, and the Hocus Pocus Hotel mystery/comedy series. Dahl currently lives in Minneapolis, Minnesota, in a haunted house.

John Sazaklis

John Sazaklis is a *New York Times* bestselling author with almost 100 children's books under his utility belt! He has also illustrated Spider-Man books, created toys for *MAD* magazine, and written for the BEN 10 animated series. John lives in New York City with his superpowered wife and daughter.

Patrycja Fabicka

Patrycja Fabicka is an illustrator with a love for magic, nature, soft colors, and storytelling. Creating cute and colorful illustrations is something that warms her heart—even during cold winter nights. She hopes that her artwork will inspire children, as she was once inspired by *The Snow Queen, Cinderella,* and other fairy tales.

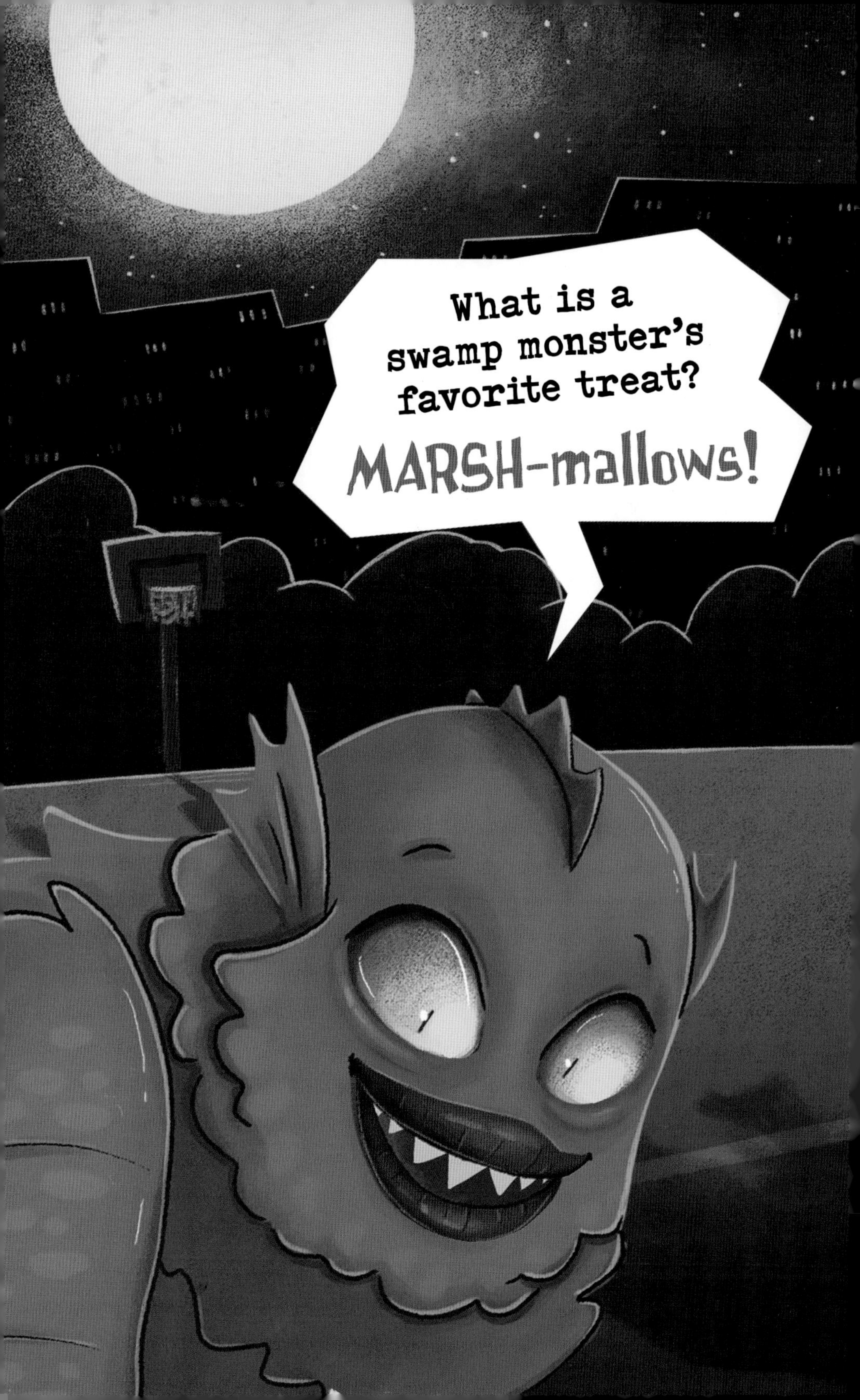
What is a swamp monster's favorite treat?
MARSH-mallows!